This book is dedicated to our family. The love and support
we receive from all is so awesome and without
each and every one, this book and everything else
we do would not be possible.

ISBN 978-1-7330470-0-5

First Printing 2019

Wonderland Industries, Inc.
1330 N. Monte Vista Ave.
Suite 15
Upland, CA 91786

www.wonderlandindustries.com

Printed in China

My Magical Unicorn Tea Party

illustrated by Katarzyna Doszla

PiXiE CRUSH

I made cupcakes and tea, and everyone came,
Birds and puppies and kitty cats, too.

7

But something was missing, and I knew what it was,
Something with magic you wouldn't find in a zoo.

I have four legs and I am truly a beautiful mare,
I have wings to fly and rainbow hair.

3

But there, on the tip of my head, pointing to the stars,
A sparkly corn shining bright from afar!

Who do you think I am? Who do you think I could be?
I am a unicorn! Flying in the sky so free!

I'd fly high over the ocean, mountains, and trees.
What is that I spot? A loving unicorn of the sea!

A Narwhal swims gently and has a horn so long and so bright.
Will you be my friend and have tea with me tonight?

Oh, what's up ahead, what's that I see?
Something shining and purring sitting high in a tree!

Why hello, little Kittycorn. How do you do?
Like me, you have a tiny horn, and lovely magic inside you.

Come along, Kittycorn, come with Narwhal and me,
We can eat cupcakes with sprinkles and sip on our tea,

There, ahead, rolling in the grass and being silly,
Little Puppycorn plays... oh yes, oh really!

Hi, Puppycorn, do you want to join us for tea?
What's that? Cupcakes, too? Yes, yes, we certainly do!

At last, back home, all of us safe and sound,
We can't forget to be princesses about to be crowned!

Our crowns have jewels that sparkle and shimmer,
It matches our corns that already glimmer!

I wish I were a magical unicorn, flying high with you,
With Kittycorn, Puppycorn and yes, Narwhal you too!

I wish you were all here with me to see,
A lovely rainbow as we finish our tea.